THE CHILDREN'S BOOK OF
AMERICA

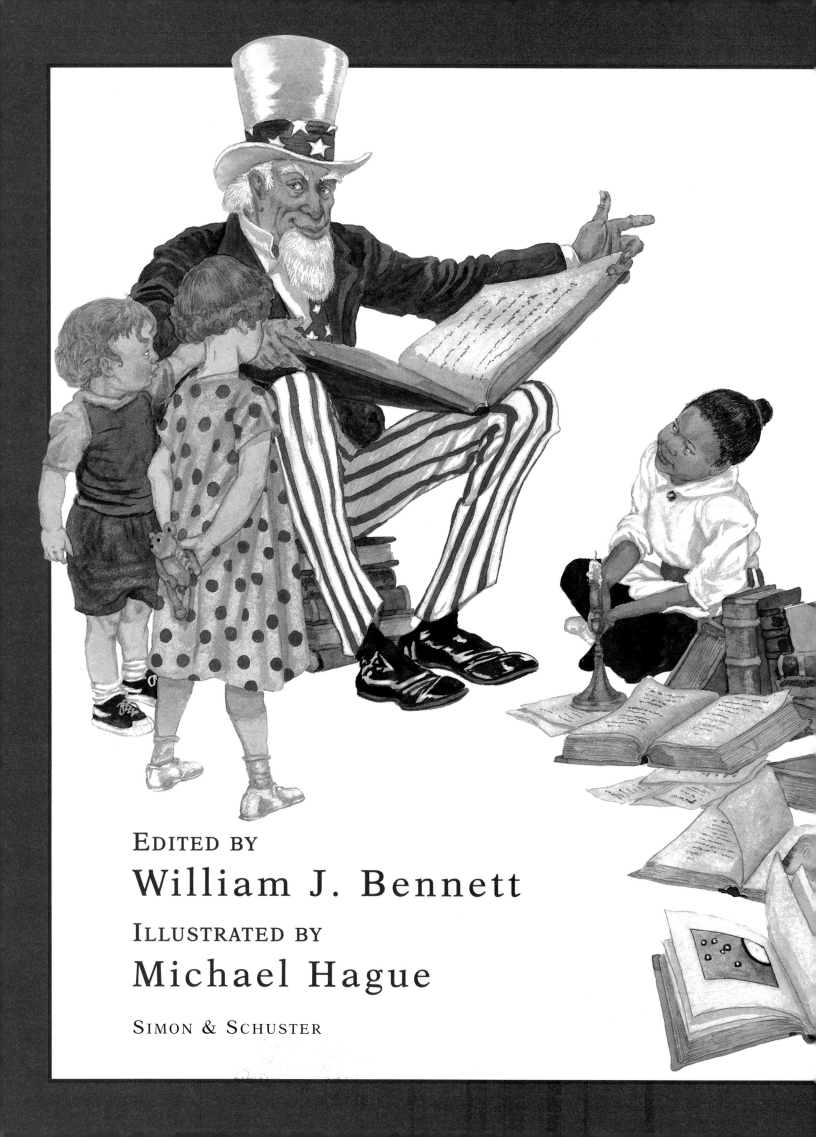

EDITED BY

William J. Bennett

ILLUSTRATED BY

Michael Hague

SIMON & SCHUSTER

THE CHILDREN'S BOOK OF
AMERICA

SIMON & SCHUSTER
Rockefeller Center
1230 Avenue of the Americas
New York, NY 10020

Designed by Amy Hill

Manufactured in the United States of America

1 3 5 7 9 10 8 6 4 2

Library of Congress Cataloging-in-Publication Data

The children's book of America/edited by William J. Bennett;
illustrated by Michael Hague
p.   cm.
Summary: Presents stories of significant events and people in American history,
patriotic songs, and American folk tales and poems
1. United States—History—Miscellanea—Juvenile literature
[1. United States—History—Miscellanea]
I. Bennett, William J. (William John), 1943– II. Hague, Michael, ill.
E178.3.C5   1998   98-15491
973—dc21   CIP
                                 AC

ISBN 0-684-84930-5

Excerpt on page 8 from "Bernard DeVoto: Historian, Critic, and Fighter,"
by Catherine Drinker Bowen, from *The Year of Decision 1846*, by Bernard DeVoto.
Copyright ©1942, 1943 by Bernard DeVoto.
Reprinted by permission of Houghton Mifflin Company.

They celebrated with games as well. The settlers and Indians held shooting contests with both guns and bows. The young men challenged each other in foot races and wrestling matches. The Englishmen did jigs for the Indians, and the Indians in turn showed off their own dances.

For three days the feast continued. The Pilgrims knew well that more days of trial and hardship lay ahead. But for now, they rejoiced together over the gifts they had received. They thanked God for bringing them across the stormy ocean and seeing them through the long, harsh winter. They thanked Him for the bountiful fruits of their labor. They gave thanks for their Indian friends. And they gave thanks for this new land, where they could worship as they pleased.

Every year we remember that long-ago feast called the First Thanksgiving. On the fourth Thursday of each November, we rejoice that friends and loved ones have gathered safely together. We celebrate the fruits of our labor. We recall that throughout our nation's past, our ancestors risked their lives so we might be free. We bow our heads in thanks for all the bounty of this land and for the many blessings we have received.

Father Junipero Serra

In 1769, the king of Spain sent explorers from Mexico to California to begin settling that vast, beautiful land. One of their leaders was a priest named Father Junipero Serra. Often the settlers' efforts seemed doomed, but Father Serra refused to give up. Time and again in American history, such perseverance has made all the difference.

A line of men and beasts crept across the scorched California desert. Spanish soldiers wiped their brows. Mules staggered under bulky loads of supplies. Indian guides trudged wearily. They were looking for a bay called San Diego, but before them the earth lay brown and empty.

In the midst of this party limped a small priest in a gray robe named Padre Junipero Serra. He was born in Spain, but even as a boy he dreamed of exploring the New World. He came not to find gold or jewels but to spread the word of God.

Padre Serra's kind, bright eyes told of a gentle soul. They also spoke of a courage that never failed. "Always go forward and never turn back" was his motto.

The padre was not a young man. He had a sore left leg, which had been bitten by an insect years before and now

hurt all the time. He set out bravely, leaning on a stick as he limped along. But before many miles, he was in great pain. The swelling went halfway up his leg until he could no longer walk. The soldiers looked at him and frowned.

"There is no way you can make it. We are sending you back to Mexico."

Padre Serra shook his head.

"I may not make it to San Diego, but it is God's will that I try," he said. "I will not turn back."

That evening he sent for the young man who took care of the mules.

"Son, can you cure my leg?" he asked. The fellow was so surprised he could barely answer.

"But father, I only know how to treat the sores on the mules," he objected.

"Then pretend I am a mule." Padre Serra smiled.

The muleteer gathered the plants he needed, made a medicine, and spread it on the priest's leg. The next morning Padre Serra could walk again. The soldiers stared in amazement.

"This man lets nothing stand in his way," they whispered to each other.

The explorers hauled themselves across the barren land. They saw nothing but rocks, thorns, and sand. They labored up and down steep slopes. They pushed through cactus thickets. Their water supply ran low. Vultures circled overhead, watching and waiting.

The soldiers clutched at their dust-parched throats. They began to argue among themselves and talked of deserting.

"If we don't find water soon, we'll die," they muttered. "Better to turn back now, before it's too late."

"God is watching over us," Padre Serra told them. "We must never give up hope."

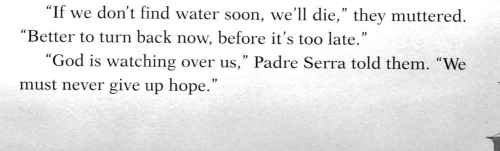

Sure enough, soon they came upon a beautiful stream. The desert gave way to more fertile lands, dotted here and there with clumps of trees.

At last they reached a place where the sea curved inland. Looking down on the wide blue bay, they spied two ships that had sailed north from Mexico to meet them. They had reached San Diego. With tears of joy they rushed to join their comrades.

But their happiness soon gave way to grim news. The ships had suffered a long, hard voyage. Many sailors had perished. More lay sick and dying. Their stores of food were running low.

The Spaniards held a council and chose a course of action. One of the ships, the *San Antonio*, would sail back to Mexico for more men and fresh supplies. The rest would try to hold on in California. The soldiers looked at one another uneasily. They knew the odds against them were growing day by day. The future looked dark.

Padre Serra put his fate in the hands of God and went straight to work. The settlers built a few crude huts where the sick could be nursed to health. One of the huts was set aside as a mission church. Padre Serra set up a cross facing the sea. From the branch of a tree he hung a bell. He called the Indians to come and hear about God.

But then followed months of hardship and disappointment. The Indians did not always come when Padre Junipero rang the mission bell. They did not know what to make of these newcomers and their strange ways. One day they attacked the mission. It broke Padre Serra's heart to see God's children fighting.

Sickness spread and more men died. Padre Junipero himself became ill. Almost all the food was gone. The men were always hungry and weak.

Every day the Spaniards looked to sea, hoping the *San Antonio* would return. But day after day there was no sign of aid. No word came from Mexico—only silence.

It seemed madness to stay any longer, and so a decision was made—they would pack up and go home. But Padre Serra begged his comrades to wait a while longer.

"In nine days it will be the Feast of Saint Joseph," he said. "Wait until then. If the *San Antonio* has not arrived, I, too, will admit defeat."

The padre's faith touched every heart. It was agreed to hang on a bit longer. Each day Padre Serra prayed, but each day the ocean lay empty. St. Joseph's Day arrived. The soldiers packed and prepared to go.

The afternoon shadows lengthened. The sun sank toward the sea.

"Have hope," Padre Serra whispered. "The day is not yet over."

The soldiers smiled at each other sadly. This man refused to give up!

Then someone pointed toward the water. A speck appeared on the horizon. The men held their breaths and watched.

"A sail! A sail!" The cry ran through the camp. It was the *San Antonio*, bringing men and food and medicine.

Was it a miracle? Those who watched Padre Serra fall to his knees and give thanks thought surely the good man's prayers had been answered.

The San Diego mission grew and flourished. It was only the first. Padre Serra and his comrades proceeded to found a string of missions along the California coast. At each one they hung a bell to chime the hour and summon all to prayer.

Some of the old missions still stand. When Americans hear the ringing of their bells, they remember the gentle little priest who limped hundreds of miles up and down California, telling of God and cheering others with these words: "Always go forward and never turn back."

The Bravery of Abigail Adams

The Revolutionary War years were a terrible and dangerous time. Many patriots had to flee their homes, and many lost everything they owned. Others suffered one of life's hardest challenges—they were torn from their loved ones. Abigail and John Adams spent many years apart during the period of our nation's founding, but their love for America and each other pulled them through.

The year was 1775, and sparks of rebellion whirled through the air. The American colonists were talking about freedom from England. British Redcoats swarmed through the streets of Boston. Patriots held secret meetings while men such as Paul Revere jumped on their horses and galloped from town to town, carrying news and warnings. Minutemen—farmers and tradesmen ready to fight on a moment's notice—shouldered their muskets and marched toward Boston. Everyone wondered if America and Britain were on the road to war.

In the village of Braintree, near Boston, Abigail Adams struggled amid the confusion and alarm. Her husband, John, was far away in Philadelphia at a meeting of the Continental Congress. There, leaders such as George Washington, Thomas Jefferson, and Benjamin Franklin were gathering to plot America's future. With John in Philadelphia, it was up to Abigail to care for the children and manage the farm alone.

There was much to do. The cows must be milked, the orchards tended, the accounts balanced. There were shirts to be sewn and pots to stir in the big kitchen fireplace. Many things were in short supply—sugar, pepper, pins—so Abigail did without them. Since the schools were closed because of the danger, the children were taught at home.

Minutemen, hungry and thirsty, tramped past the door, and Abigail gave them food and drink. Patriot families, fleeing Boston, poured into the countryside. Abigail spread blankets on the floor and gave shelter to as many as she could.

Abigail loved her husband and wanted him at her side in these unnerving times. But she also knew that America needed him for a while.

Almost every day she wrote to John, telling him about the children and the farm. She reported on the troubles in Boston and sent him her love and prayers.

"Good night. With thoughts of thee I close my eyes. Angels guard and protect thee."

All around her, Abigail could see and hear signs of danger. The countryside was filled with the sounds of men marching, drums beating, church bells ringing in alarm. Neighbors took sides against one another. Rumors spread like wildfire. There was news of bloodshed at Lexington and Concord, talk of fresh British troops sailing into Boston, warnings that the Redcoats were marching this way to arrest rebellious Patriots.

"In case of real danger," John wrote, "fly to the woods with our children."

Abigail responded bravely.

"Courage I know we have in abundance, conduct I hope we shall not want," she wrote, "but gunpowder—where shall we get a sufficient supply?"

Early one morning, before the sun rose, Abigail woke to a distant rumble. For a moment she lay still, listening for what she thought must be thunder. The deep booming came again, rolling across the hills from Boston. She leaped out of bed and dressed hastily by candlelight.

The noise woke her young son, Johnny, too. Taking him by the hand, Abigail climbed through orchards to the top of a nearby hill. They held their breaths and peered through the graying dawn.

Off toward Boston, smoke hung on the horizon. A faraway fiery glow filled the hazy air. Distant rockets burst in the sky and cannon blasts shattered the early morning stillness.

"What is it, Mother?" Johnny asked.

Abigail felt his eyes upon her, wide and uncertain, and she shuddered, for she knew it was the start of a long and terrible struggle for liberty—and that America's fate now hung in the balance.

Several days later in far-off Philadelphia, a gloomy John Adams sat in his boardinghouse room, his spirits sinking like a stone. He had just received a letter from Abigail telling of a terrible battle at Bunker Hill. Many brave men had fallen on both sides.

John was sick with worry about his family. Were they safe? Did they have enough food to eat? Where would they go if the Redcoats ran them out of their home?

He despaired at the slow work of the Continental Congress. There was so much squabbling among its members. How were the colonies to govern themselves? How could the rag-tag Patriot army stand up to the king's soldiers? Where would George Washington find enough men and muskets to fight?

Tired and lonely, John rose and paced the hot room. A frown creased his forehead. Perhaps the fight for liberty was a hopeless cause. Then his eyes fell on a few words in Abigail's letter.

"The race is not to the swift, nor the battle to the strong, but the God of Israel is he that giveth strength and power unto his people. Trust in him at all times. . . ."

Tears of love and pride sprang to his eyes. He thought of his wife's courage and faith. Even as danger swirled all around her, she somehow carried on with the task of counseling her husband, protecting her family, and aiding the Patriot cause.

The clouds of doubt parted. With such bravery and devotion, nothing was impossible. John Adams knew the colonies could win their freedom. With fresh strength he picked up his pen and went back to the work of founding a new and great nation.

"Yankee Doodle"

The Spirit of '76 echoes in this song. British troops originally sang it to make fun of the shabby Colonial army, but the hard-fighting Americans liked the tune so much, they made it their own during the Revolutionary War. "Yankee" was a nickname for New Englanders, "doodle" meant a foolish fellow, and "macaroni" was slang for a dandy who liked to dress in style.

Yankee Doodle went to town,
A-ridin' on a pony,
Stuck a feather in his hat
And called it macaroni.

Chorus:
Yankee Doodle, keep it up,
Yankee Doodle Dandy,
Mind the music and the step
And with the girls be handy.

Father and I went down to camp
Along with Captain Gooding,
And there we saw the men and boys
As thick as hasty pudding.

Yankee·Doodle·went·to·town·

And there was Captain Washington
Upon a slapping stallion,
A-giving orders to his men,
I guess there were a million.

And there I saw a wooden drum
With heads made out of leather,
They knocked upon it with some sticks
To call the folks together.

And then they'd fife away like fun
And play on cornstalk fiddles,
And some had ribbons red as blood
All bound around their middles.

Uncle Sam came there to change
Some pancakes and some onions
For 'lasses cakes to carry home
To give his wife and young ones.

But I can't tell you half I saw,
They kept up such a smother,
So I took my hat off, made a bow,
And scampered home to mother.

A·ridin'·on·a·pony

Westward with Lewis and Clark

The very first journey across our country and back took more than two years!
Travel is faster these days, but blazing new trails is still the American way.

Two hundred years ago, most of this country was a wild, unexplored land that stretched toward the setting sun. Great rivers flowed out of the western frontiers, but where did they come from? There were rumors of rugged mountains, but how high did they reach? Somewhere beyond the mountains lay the Pacific Ocean. How far away was the sea? No one knew.

One morning in 1804, a clumsy-looking barge with a big square sail pushed up the wide Missouri River. Behind it came two long sturdy canoes called pirogues. All three boats were loaded with men and supplies. On the deck of the barge, two men stood talking. Their names were Captain Meriwether Lewis and Captain William Clark. They were setting out to do what no one had ever done before—travel across America to the great Pacific Ocean.

Washington, D.C.

St. Louis

UNITED STATES

President Thomas Jefferson was sending this party to explore the boundless frontier. He wanted Lewis and Clark to find a path that would lead across the country. So this brave group of adventurers said goodbye to their friends and loved ones and started west into uncharted lands.

Progress up the Missouri River was hard and slow. Sometimes the explorers pushed the barge upstream with long poles. Sometimes they trudged along the riverbanks, towing the boat with a long rope. Captain Lewis and Captain Clark took turns scouting the land, collecting leaves, flowers, rocks, and even dinosaur bones to send back to Thomas Jefferson. They drew maps of their route so that others could someday follow.

The prairies stretched as far as the eye could see. The land teemed with deer, turkeys, and geese, which the explorers hunted for dinner. At night, the sky filled with blazing stars. Wolves howled. Bears rustled in the bushes. Sometimes, when the men rose in the gray dawn, they shook rattlesnakes from their blankets.

Soon they reached Indian territory, where tribes such as the Otoes, the Omahas, and the Sioux lived. Captain Lewis and Captain Clark held councils with the Indians. The proud chiefs came dressed in their finery—their skin painted yellow and red and green, their hair decorated with feathers and porcupine quills, their throats gleaming with bear-claw necklaces. Sometimes the Indians welcomed these newcomers as friends. Some tribes, however, feared that these strangers came to rob them of their lands. Always Lewis and Clark kept their eyes open and their guns within reach, ready for any surprise.

On the explorers pushed. Great plains spread before them, covered with herds of buffalo, elk, and antelope. Prairie dogs scampered into their holes. Beavers splashed by the river's shores. The land's size and bounty seemed to go on forever.

But now cold weather approached. Ice began to float down the river and the northern lights danced overhead at night. The tired explorers halted to build a winter camp. They crawled under buffalo blankets and snored while the blizzards piled snowdrifts all around their log cabins.

One day a French trader named Charbonneau arrived at the little outpost. Lewis and Clark decided to make him a part of their expedition since he spoke the Indians' language. With him came his young Shoshoni wife, Sacagawea, a name that meant "bird woman." That winter Sacagawea gave birth to a son, Jean Baptiste.

At last the snows melted and it was time to start out again. The big barge was loaded with everything the explorers had gathered so far—Indian clothes, animal skins, plants, insects, even live birds and a prairie dog—and sent back downstream to President Jefferson. The explorers, meanwhile, headed farther west. With the two pirogues and six new canoes they pushed upstream, into the unknown.

Sacagawea pushed steadily forward, too, carrying little Baptiste on a papoose board. It did not take her long to show her courage and quick thinking. One day a squall overturned one of the pirogues. The boat filled with water. Clothing, equipment, medicine, and all sorts of valuable instruments floated away. With her infant strapped to her back, Sacagawea plucked the supplies from the icy river. If they had been lost, the explorers might have been forced to turn back.

"If Fort McHenry can stand, the city is safe," Francis Scott Key muttered to himself. He stared anxiously through the smoke to see if the flag was still flying.

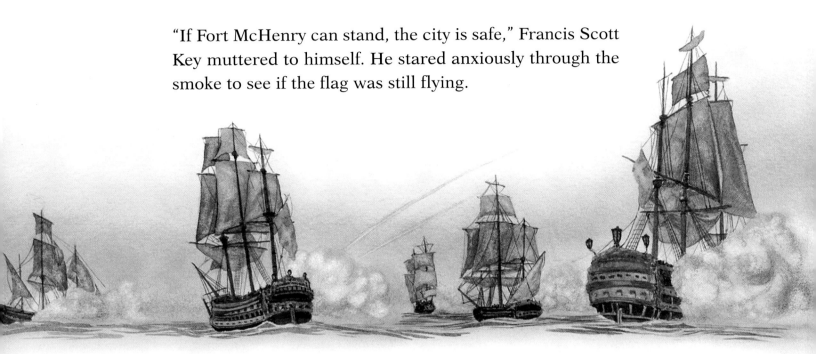

The young Washington lawyer was watching the battle from a little American vessel floating with the British ships. He had sailed out to the British fleet under a flag of truce before the fighting began. A friend had been seized prisoner by the British, and Key went to ask for his release. The British commander agreed, but he would not let Key return to Baltimore with any information he might have picked up. "Until the battle is over, you and your boat stay here," he ordered.

Key had no choice but to wait it out, pacing the deck and hoping the fort could hold out. The firing went on and on. As long as the daylight lasted, he could catch glimpses of the Stars and Stripes through the clouds of smoke. When night came, he could still see the banner now and then by the blaze of the cannon.

Finally, toward daybreak, the firing stopped. Key strained to see if the flag was still flying. "Could the fort have held out?" he wondered.

The faint gray of dawn crept into the sky. He could see that some flag was flying—but was it American or British? Who held Fort McHenry?

More and more eagerly he gazed. It grew lighter. A sudden breath of wind caught the banner and it floated out on

the breeze. This was no English flag; it was Mary Pickersgill's Stars and Stripes, still waving through the smoke and mist! Fort McHenry had stood, and the city was safe!

Overcome with joy, Key snatched an old letter from his pocket. Still watching the flag, he began scribbling a few lines on its back.

The British departed and the little American boat sailed back to the city. Key gave a copy of the poem he had just written to his brother-in-law, who had helped defend the fort. His brother-in-law sent it to a printer and had it struck off on some handbills. Before the ink was dry, the printer snatched one up and hurried to a tavern where many patriots were assembling.

"Listen to this!" he cried, and he read the verse to the crowd.

"Sing it! Sing it!" the whole company cried. Someone mounted a chair and sang the poem to an old tune. The song caught on at once. Halls, theaters, and houses soon rang with its strains as the British fleet disappeared over the horizon.

The years passed, and Francis Scott Key's words found a place in his fellow citizens' hearts. They became the anthem of a nation that stands always for freedom, just as the Stars and Stripes stood through that perilous fight so long ago.

"The Star Spangled Banner"

O say, can you see by the dawn's early light,
What so proudly we hailed at the twilight's last gleaming,
Whose broad stripes and bright stars, through the perilous fight
O'er the ramparts we watch'd were so gallantly streaming?
And the rockets' red glare, the bombs bursting in air,
Gave proof through the night that our flag was still there.
O say, does that Star Spangled Banner yet wave
O'er the land of the free and the home of the brave?

Johnny Appleseed

John Chapman's simple, giving life made him a legend in his own day. When news of his death in 1845 reached Washington, Sam Houston stood up in Congress and said: "Farewell, dear old eccentric heart. Your labor has been a labor of love, and generations yet unborn will rise up and call you blessed." This humble pioneer's spirit lives on in the lore of Johnny Appleseed.

There's a wanderer, they say, in the Ohio Valley. He comes by at apple blossom time. Get out of bed early, just as the sun rises, and you might see smoke hanging over the orchard as his breakfast fire dies low. Wait a while longer and a breeze comes rustling through the trees. The old farmers wink and smile.

"Here he comes, waking the blossoms to a new spring," they say. "That's Johnny Appleseed passing by."

John Chapman was his real name. Folks in Pittsburgh say he had a big flowering orchard there, way back when the country was new. Day after day he sat on his fence and watched covered wagons rolling by, full of pioneer families, headed west.

"Rough lives await them, full of hardship and toil," he thought. "What can I do to help?"

He watched the wagons go rumbling by and an idea took root in his mind. It grew and grew until it turned into a plan. So he filled a bag with apple seeds and slung it over his shoulder. Then he wandered away.

John walked through woods filled with oaks and hickories. He crossed fields where tall grasses waved in the wind.

Every once in a while, beside a stream or in a clearing, he would pause and untie his bag. With a pointed stick he dug holes, then stooped and planted some seeds. He covered them well, knowing they would grow in the sunshine and rain.

When the wagons came rolling west, the seedlings were green and strong. He dug them up carefully and gave them to pioneer families.

"Set them in the earth, and someday you'll harvest nature's jewels!" he told them. "Apples! Apple butter! Apple sauce! Apple cider! Jelly and pie!"

The settlers smiled and took the seedlings gladly. They planted orchards beside their new homes.

People began to call him Johnny Appleseed.

On he went. When his shoes wore out, he walked in his bare feet. Whenever he tore a hole in his shirt, he just took his needle and thread and sewed on a patch. For a hat he wore the old tin pot he used to cook his dinner.

"This is all I need," he would say. "God has made me rich, for I'm helping my fellow man."

Far and wide he traveled, across hills and valleys, through summer storms and winter snow. When night fell, he stretched out on a hillside. A mound of moss was his pillow, the starry sky his roof. When morning broke he would rise and walk on.

His orchards spread across the frontier, and so did Johnny Appleseed's fame.

Sometimes an Indian came striding along and walked with him through the wilds. But more often than not, he walked alone. Then, they say, the birds perched on his shoulder and deer ate from his hand. Sometimes he would pause and play with bear cubs while the mother bear looked on.

When a log cabin came into view, Johnny Appleseed was always welcome to rest his weary feet. Around the big fireplace the family would gather. The children lay on the floor, and Johnny would pull his Bible from his coffee sack shirt.

"Here's news straight from Heaven," he'd say. He would read of Noah's ark or the Sermon on the Mount.

His voice was so gentle and his smile so kind, they always asked him to stay awhile. He'd shake his head. "I've got work to do. Got to be on my way."

Ohio filled up with fences and barns and orchards.

"Time to be moving on," Johnny said. He headed west, planting seeds for the country as it moved west, too.

Some say he came to rest in Indiana, beneath the bough of an apple tree. Others say he just kept walking. Who knows how far he got? All across America—in the hills of Tennessee, the plains of Nebraska, the slopes of the Rockies, the wide valleys of California—people point to orchards and say: "Johnny Appleseed planted these trees."

Maybe he's been your way, too.

General Lee reached out and grasped the soldier's hand firmly. Looking into his eyes, he said softly, "My son, I hope you will soon be well."

The Union soldier stared back. The expression on General Lee's face was so weary and kind that he knew he would never forget it if he lived a thousand years. There he was, beaten, retiring from a field that had cost him and his army their last hope, and yet he stopped to comfort a wounded foe who had taunted him as he passed by!

General Lee rode slowly away. His words, however, lodged in the soldier's heart and stayed there long after the war ended.

Margaret of New Orleans

ADAPTED FROM SARAH CONE BRYANT

Throughout our history, countless people have come to this land of opportunity and receiving much, have given even more in return. Margaret Haughery was one such immigrant. Her life, modest and compelling, is a reminder that charity is among our most honored national traits.

If you ever go to beautiful New Orleans, someone might take you down to the old part of the city along the wide Mississippi River and show you a statue that stands there. It depicts a woman sitting in a low chair, with her arms around a child who leans against her. The woman is not very pretty. She wears thick shoes and a plain dress. She is stout and short, and her face is square-chinned. But her eyes look at you like your mother's.

This is the statue of a woman named Margaret. Her whole name was Margaret Haughery, but no one in New Orleans remembers her by it, any more than you would think of your sister or your best friend by her full name. She is just Margaret. Born across the ocean in Ireland more than 150 years ago, she came to America when she was just a little girl and grew up here. Her statue is one of the first ever made in our country in honor of a woman.

As a young woman Margaret was all alone in the world. She was poor but strong, and she knew how to work. All day, from morning until evening, she ironed clothes in a laundry. And every day, as she worked by the window, she saw the little children from the nearby orphanage working and playing. They had no mothers or fathers of their own to take care of them. Margaret knew they needed a good friend.

You would hardly think that a poor woman who worked in a laundry could be much of a friend to so many children. But Margaret was. She went straight to the kind Sisters who ran the orphanage and told them she wanted to help the little ones.

So she gave part of her wages every week to the orphanage. She worked so hard that she was able to save some money, too. With this, she bought two cows and a delivery cart. She carried milk to her customers in the little cart every morning. As she went along, she asked for leftover food from hotels and rich houses, and brought it back in the cart to the hungry children in the orphanage. In the very hardest times, that was often all the food the children had.

In spite of her giving, Margaret was so careful and so good at business that she was able to buy more cows and earn more money. With this, she helped build a home for orphan babies. She called it her baby house.

After a time, Margaret had a chance to take over a bakery, and then she became a bread woman instead of a milk woman. She carried the bread just as she had carried the milk, in her cart. And still she kept giving money to the orphanage.

Then a great war came, the Civil War. In all the trouble and fear of that time, Margaret drove her cart. Somehow she always had enough bread to give to the hungry soldiers and to her babies, besides what she sold. And despite all this, she earned enough so that when the war was over she built a big steam factory to make her bread.

By this time everybody in the city knew her. The children all over New Orleans loved her. The businessmen were proud of her. The poor people all came to her for advice. She used to sit at the open door of her office in a calico gown and a little shawl and give a good word to everybody, rich or poor.

Margaret grew old and, by and by, one day she died. When it was time to read her will, people found that, even with all her giving, she had still saved a great deal of money—and she had left every cent of it to the orphanages of the city. Each one of them was given something. Whether the children were boys or girls, white or black, Jews or Christians, made no difference, for Margaret always said, "They are all orphans alike." Her splendid will was signed with an *X* instead of a name, for Margaret had never learned to read or write.

The people of New Orleans said, "She was a mother to the motherless. She was a friend to those who had no friends. She had wisdom greater than schools can teach. We will not let her memory go from us." So they made a statue of her, just as she used to look sitting in her office door or driving in her own little cart. And there it stands today, in memory of the great love and the great power of plain Margaret Haughery of New Orleans.

"Home on the Range"

This song has been called the cowboy's national anthem. Here is the America of wide-open spaces and boundless optimism—the land where seldom is heard a discouraging word.

Oh, give me a home where the buffalo roam,
Where the deer and the antelope play,
Where seldom is heard a discouraging word,
And the skies are not cloudy all day.

Chorus:
Home, home on the range,
Where the deer and the antelope play,
Where seldom is heard a discouraging word,
And the skies are not cloudy all day.

Where the air is so pure, the zephyrs so free,
The breezes so balmy and light,
That I would not exchange my home on the range
For all the cities so bright.

How often at night when the heavens are bright
With the light of the glittering stars,
Have I stood here amazed and asked as I gazed
If their glory exceeds that of ours.

Oh, give me a land where the bright diamond sand
Flows leisurely down the stream,
Where the graceful white swan goes gliding along
Like a maid in a heavenly dream.

John Henry and the Steam Drill

Some say this race between man and machine really took place in the 1870s in West Virginia, although no one can say for sure. But the story and ballad of John Henry remind us of a great American tradition: pride and pleasure in work.

Folks say John Henry was born to be a steel-driving man. His twelve-pound hammer whirled round his shoulders like the wind. When it fell, it crashed like a thunderclap. When it hit steel, sparks rained like lightning.

John Henry lived in the days when something mighty big was happening in America. From coast to coast, men were building railroads—great railroads like the Union Pacific, the Illinois Central, and the Chesapeake and Ohio. John Henry helped lay the tracks. Sometimes he drove big steel spikes into the cross-ties to hold the rails in place. Other times he hammered long steel drills into rock to cut tunnels through the mountains. After he drilled a hole, the blasting crews packed it with dynamite, lit a fuse, and blew the rock to pieces.